ROBOT GALAXY®

The Brotherhood Returns

WORTHWHILE ADVENTURES

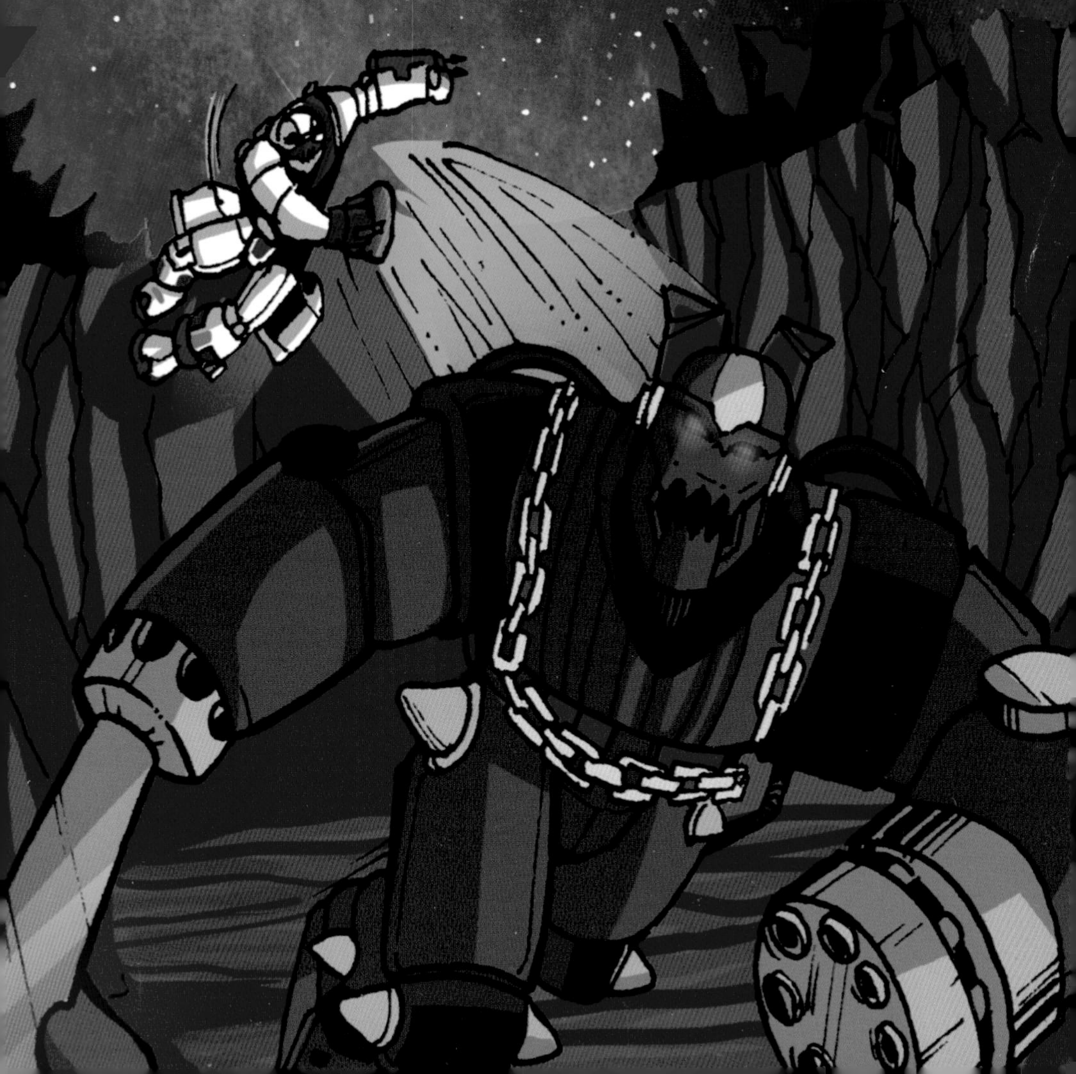

The Brotherhood Returns

Written by Rob Kurtz

Pencils and Colors by Brian Miroglio

Inks by Alberto Aprea

www.MyWorthwhileBooks.com
www.RobotGalaxy.com

ISBN: 978-1-60010-498-5   12 11 10 09   1 2 3 4 5

Based on the ROBOTGALAXY® concept created by Oliver Mitchell. Characters created by Rob Kurtz and Oliver Mitchell. Story by Rob Kurtz. Edited by Kris Oprisko. Chief Executive Officer of The Robot Factory: Ken Pilot.

ROBOTGALAXY® #1: THE BROTHERHOOD RETURNS. ROBOTGALAXY is a trademark owned by The Robot Factory, LLC with offices at 41 Union Square West, Suite 808, New York, NY 10003. The ROBOTGALAXY and its logo and all related characters are trademarks of ROBOTGALAXY and are used with permission. The ROBOTGALAXY logo is registered in the U.S. Patent and Trademarks Office. Any similarities to persons living or dead is purely coincidental.

Worthwhile Adventures, a division of Idea and Design Works, LLC.
Editorial offices: 5080 Santa Fe Street, San Diego, CA 92109.
Printed in Korea.

Worthwhile Adventures does not read or accept unsolicited submissions of ideas, stories, or artwork.

Jonas Publishing, Publisher: Howard Jonas
IDW, CEO: Ted Adams • IDW, Senior Graphic Artist: Robbie Robbins

& JONAS PUBLISHING

PRESENT:

WORTHWHILE ADVENTURES

ROBOT GALAXY®

1

The Brotherhood Returns

WORTHWHILE
ADVENTURES

At a lab in New Mexico,
a scientist built an amazing robot.

It had two parts:

a brave part to make discoveries;
a determined part to fight in battles.
Twin powers in one robot.

The robot was sent into space
on a mission to Saturn.

But as it approached
the Seventh Ring of Saturn,
there was a giant explosion.

It split into two robots. . . .

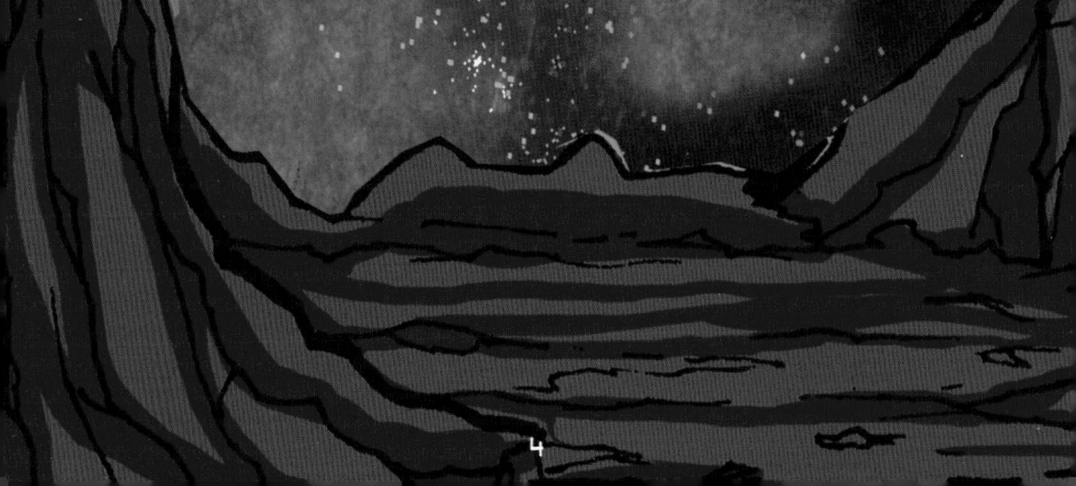

CJ-531

CREATED: 1948.
LOCATION:
Los Alamos,
New Mexico,
Earth.
BODY: Blue and
white.
EYES: Green.
TRAITS: Logic,
bravery, loyalty.

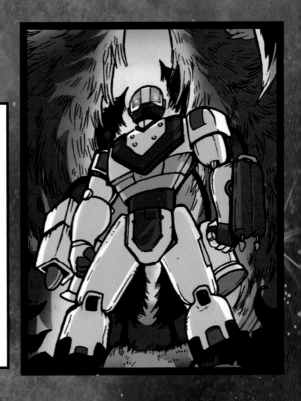

RAH

CREATED: 1948.
LOCATION:
Los Alamos,
New Mexico, Earth.
BODY: Black.
EYES: Red.
TRAITS: Violence,
strength, jealousy.

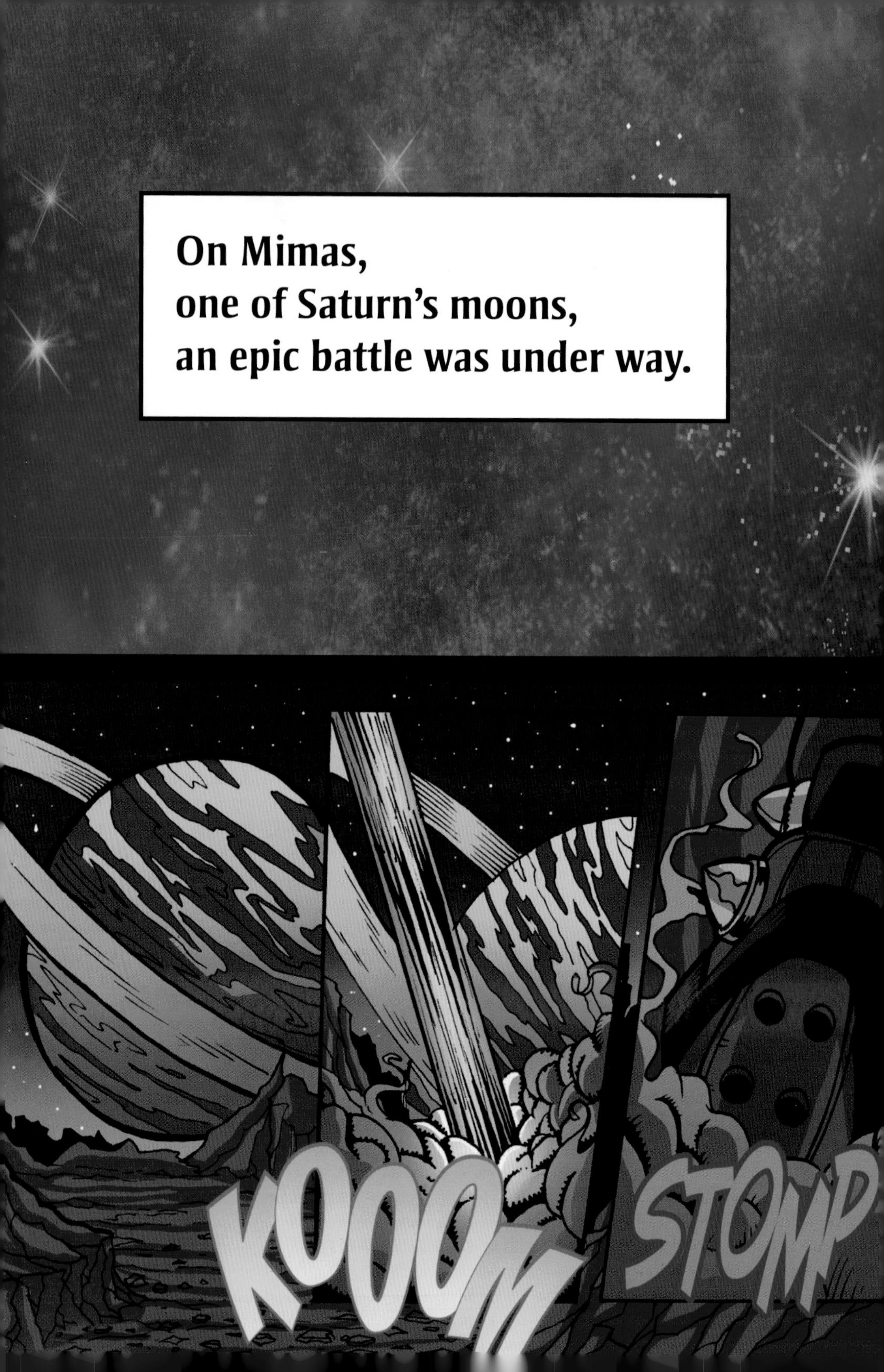
On Mimas,
one of Saturn's moons,
an epic battle was under way.
KOOOM
STOMP

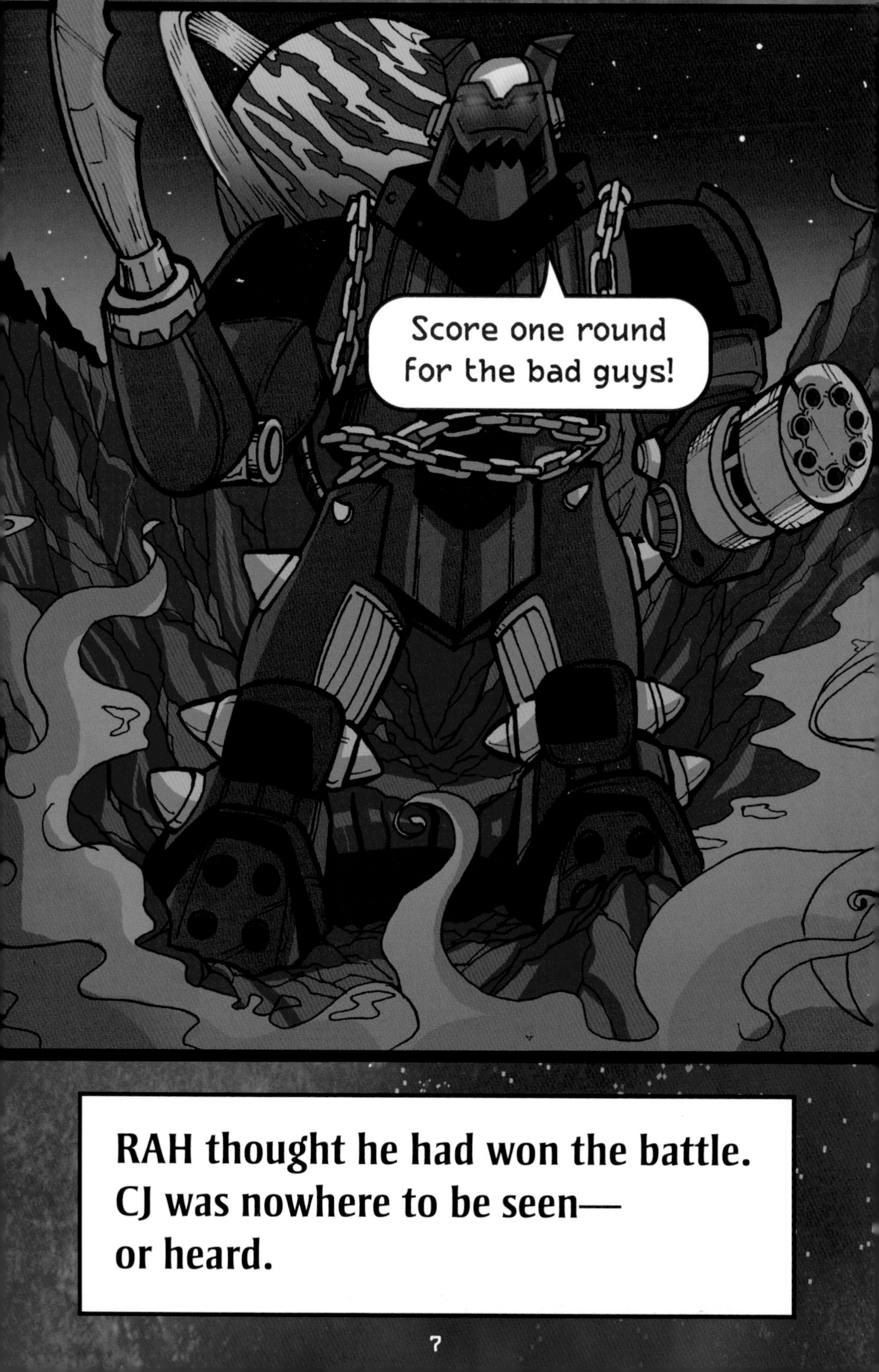
Score one round for the bad guys!

RAH thought he had won the battle. CJ was nowhere to be seen—or heard.

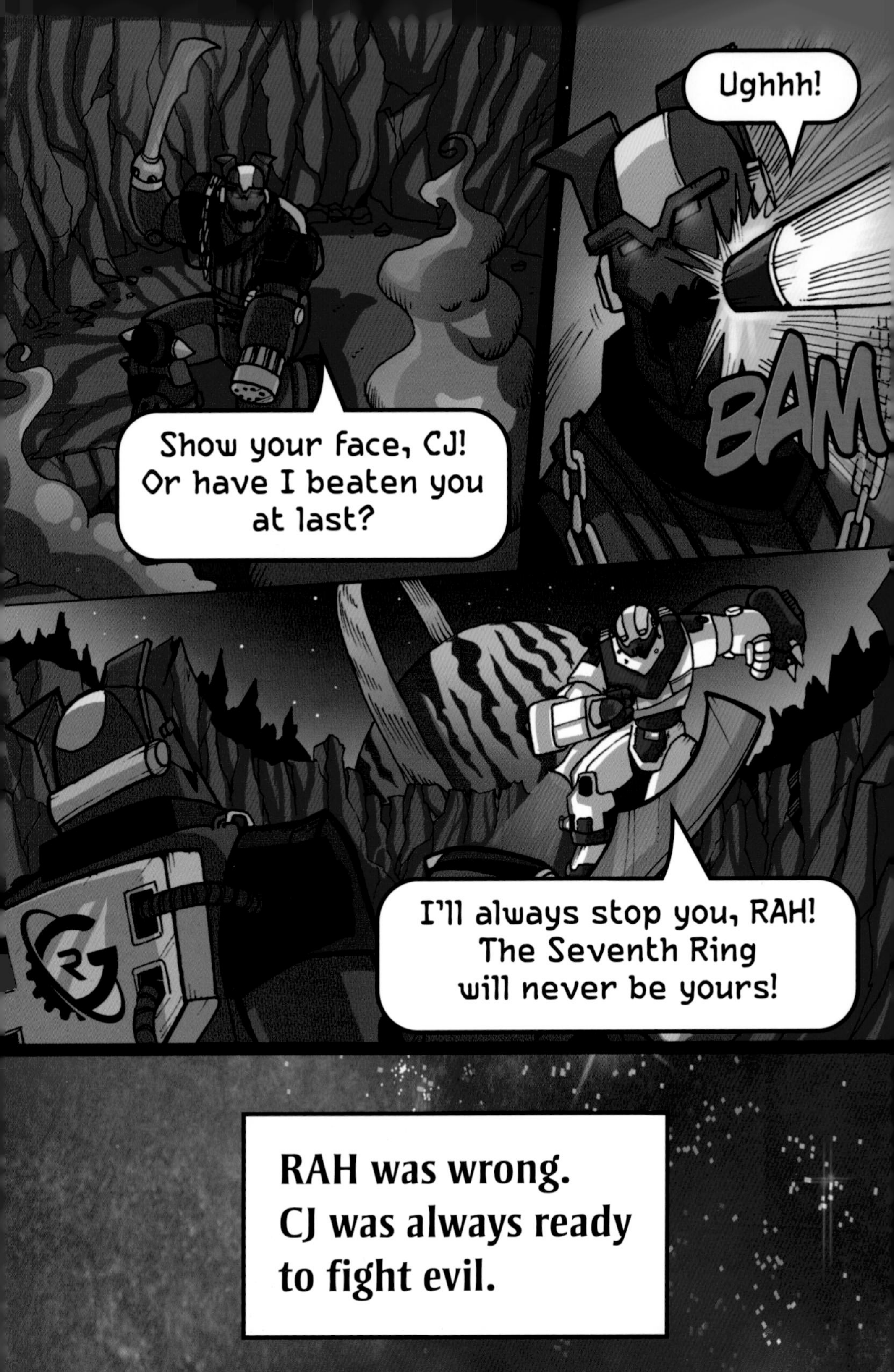
Show your face, CJ! Or have I beaten you at last?
Ughhh!
BAM
I'll always stop you, RAH! The Seventh Ring will never be yours!
RAH was wrong.
CJ was always ready
to fight evil.

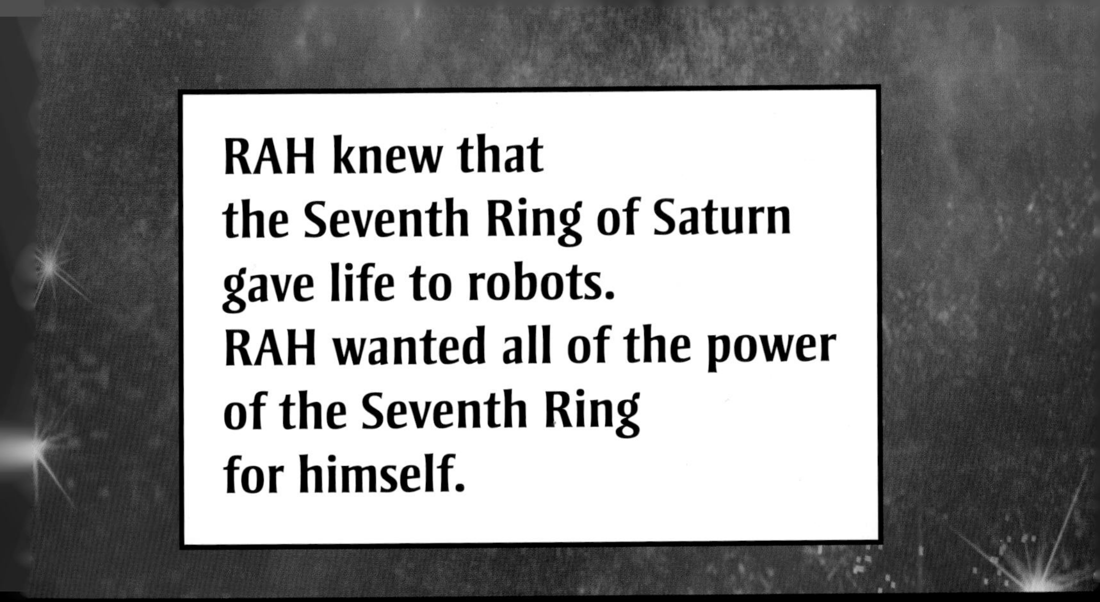
RAH knew that the Seventh Ring of Saturn gave life to robots. RAH wanted all of the power of the Seventh Ring for himself.

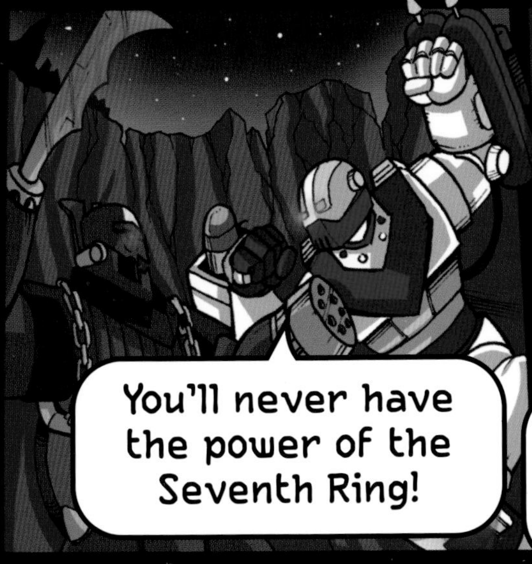
You'll never have the power of the Seventh Ring!

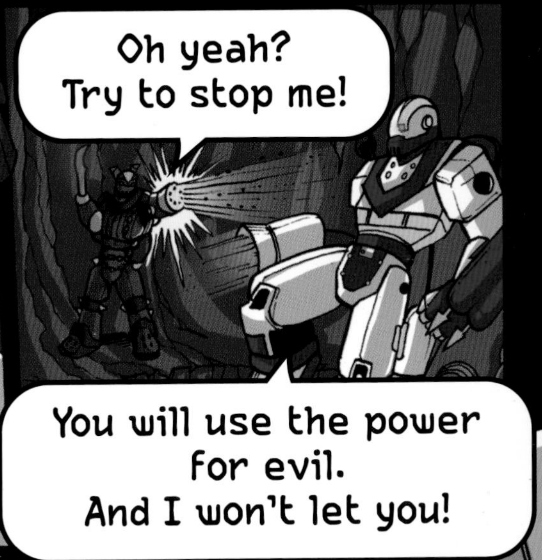
Oh yeah? Try to stop me!
You will use the power for evil. And I won't let you!

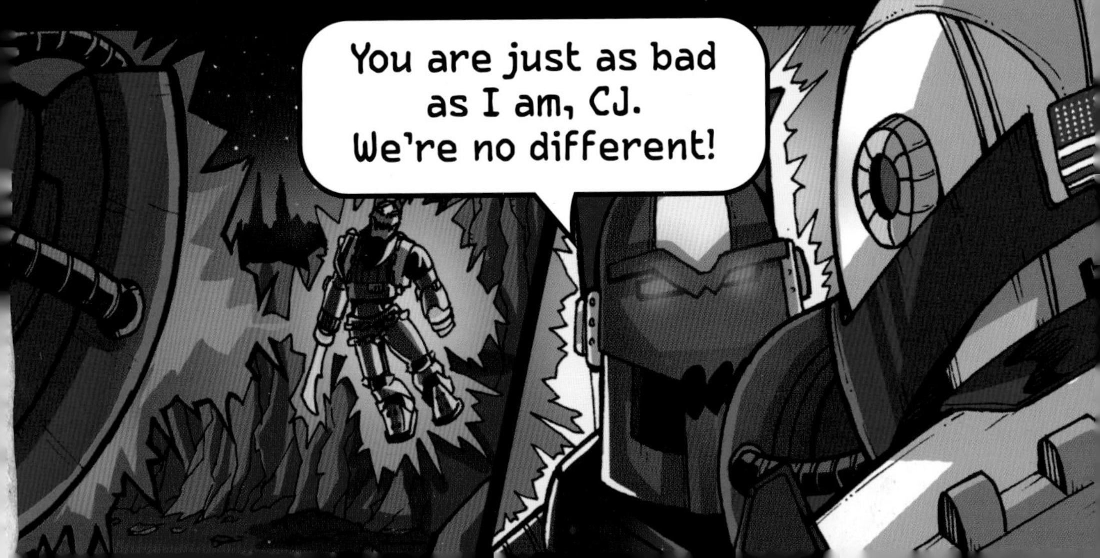
You are just as bad as I am, CJ. We're no different!

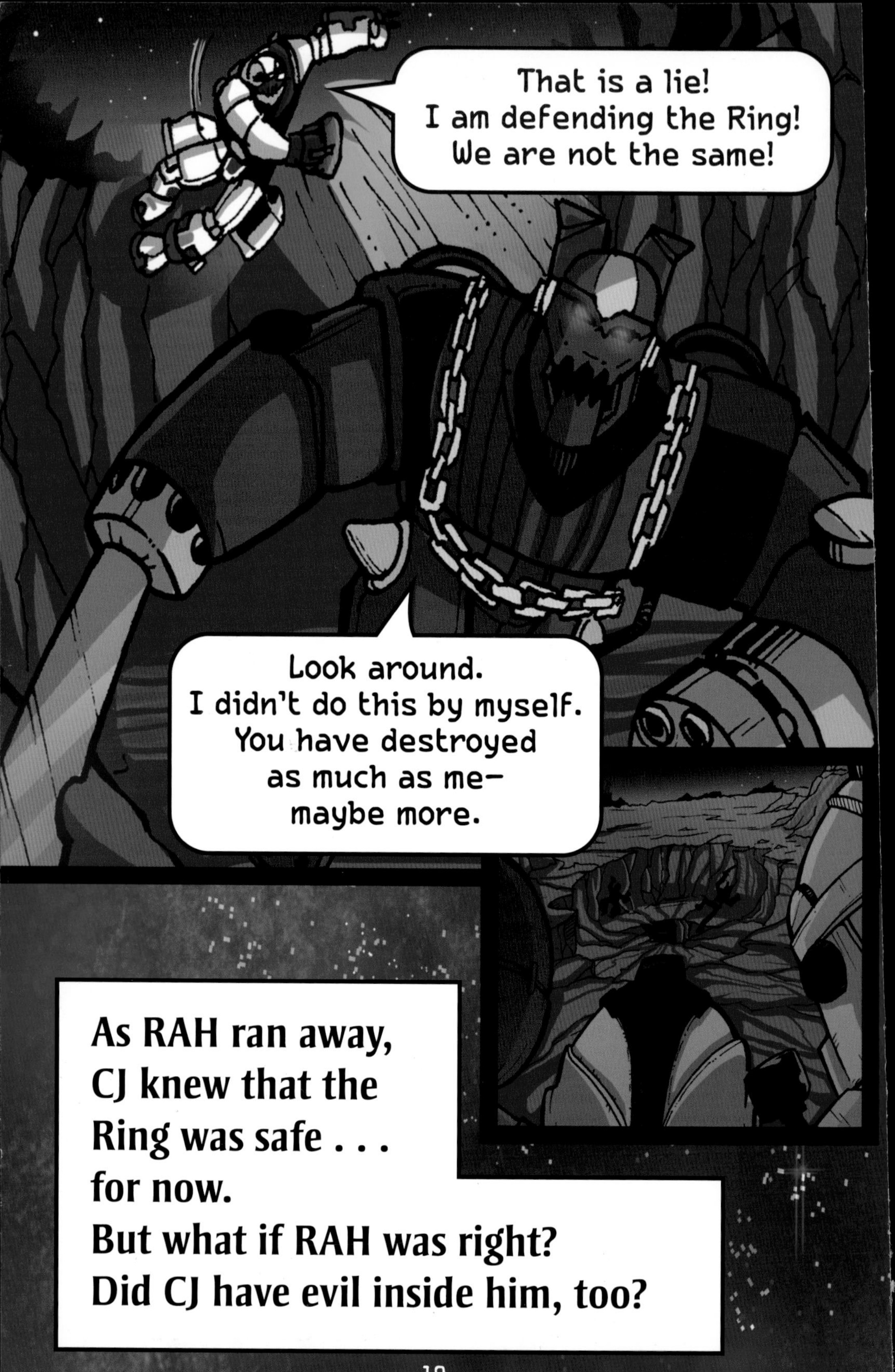
That is a lie! I am defending the Ring! We are not the same!
Look around. I didn't do this by myself. You have destroyed as much as me— maybe more.
As RAH ran away, CJ knew that the Ring was safe . . . for now. But what if RAH was right? Did CJ have evil inside him, too?

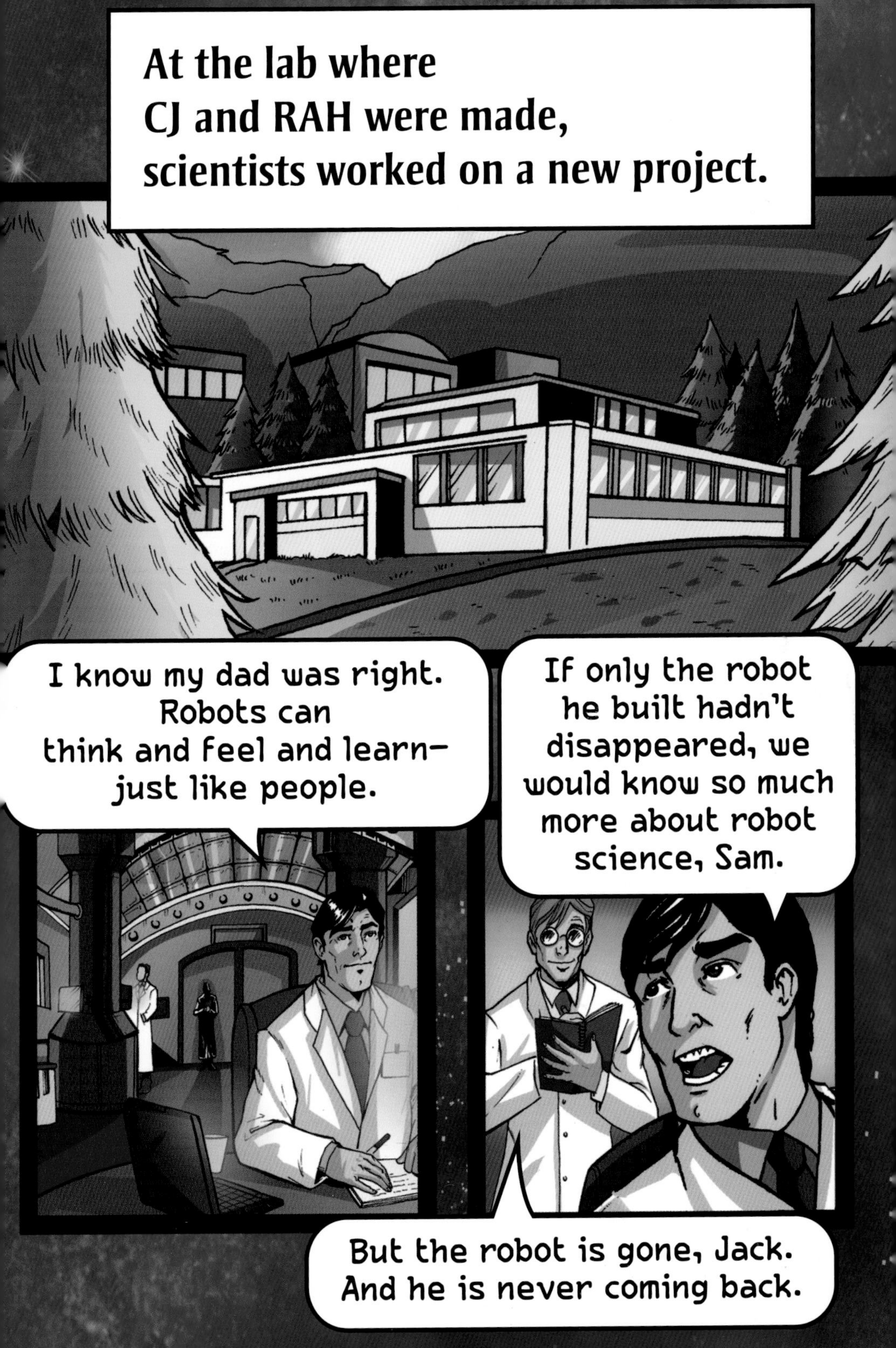
At the lab where CJ and RAH were made, scientists worked on a new project.
I know my dad was right. Robots can think and feel and learn— just like people.
If only the robot he built hadn't disappeared, we would know so much more about robot science, Sam.
But the robot is gone, Jack. And he is never coming back.

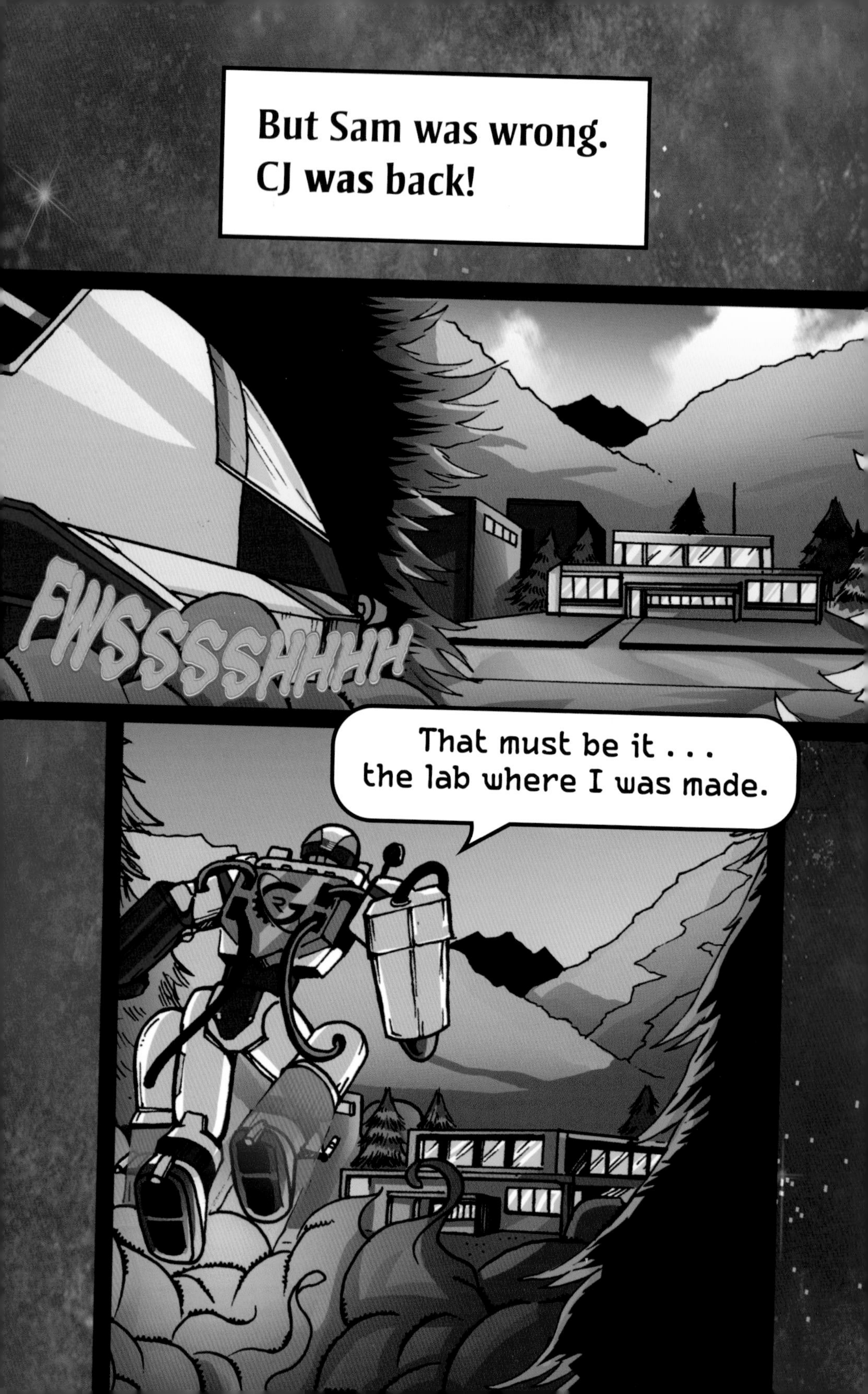
But Sam was wrong.
CJ was back!
FWSSSSHHHH
That must be it . . . the lab where I was made.

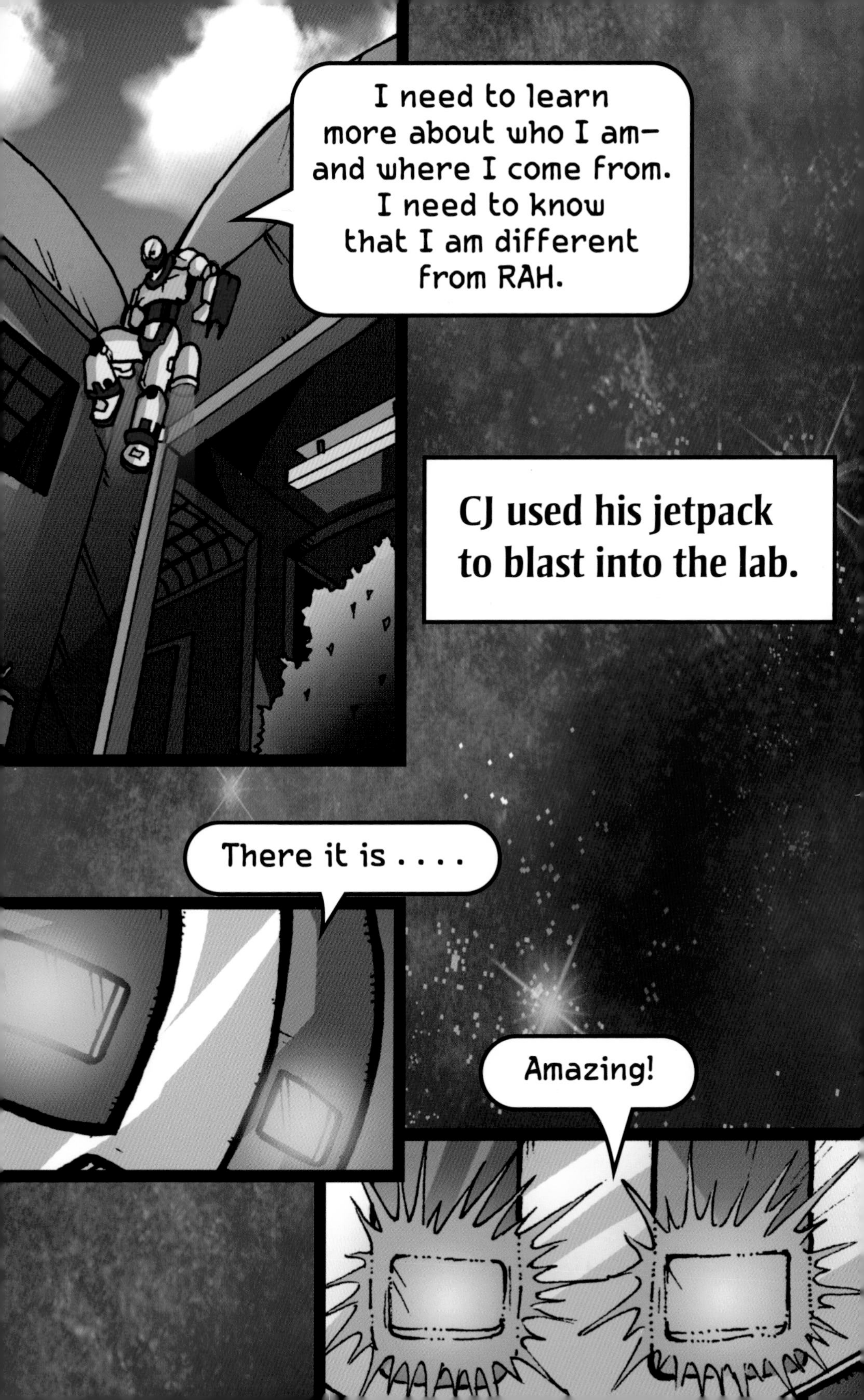
I need to learn more about who I am—and where I come from. I need to know that I am different from RAH.
CJ used his jetpack to blast into the lab.
There it is . . . .
Amazing!

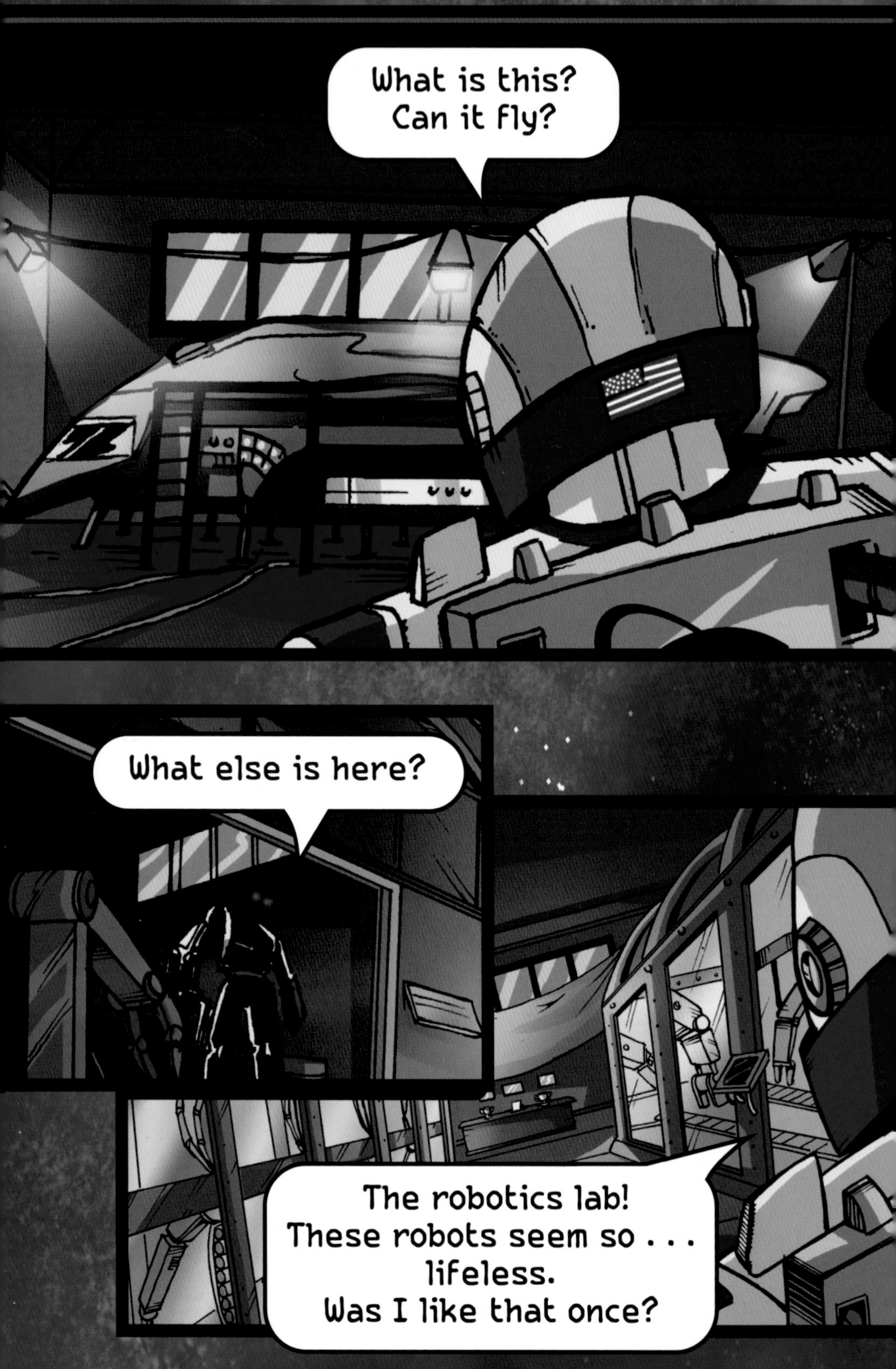
What is this? Can it fly?
What else is here?
The robotics lab! These robots seem so . . . lifeless. Was I like that once?

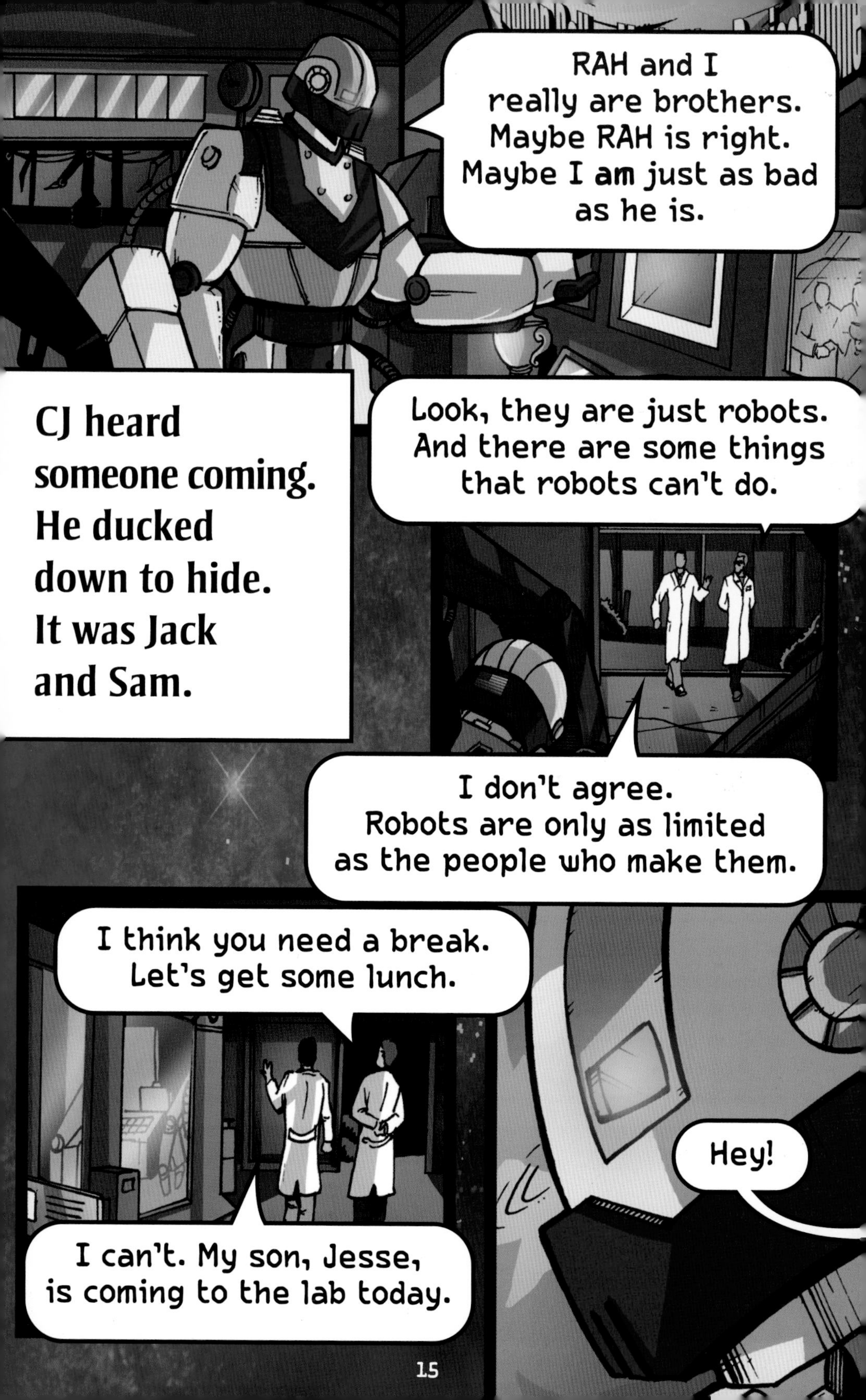
RAH and I really are brothers. Maybe RAH is right. Maybe I am just as bad as he is.
CJ heard someone coming. He ducked down to hide. It was Jack and Sam.
Look, they are just robots. And there are some things that robots can't do.
I don't agree. Robots are only as limited as the people who make them.
I think you need a break. Let's get some lunch.
I can't. My son, Jesse, is coming to the lab today.
Hey!

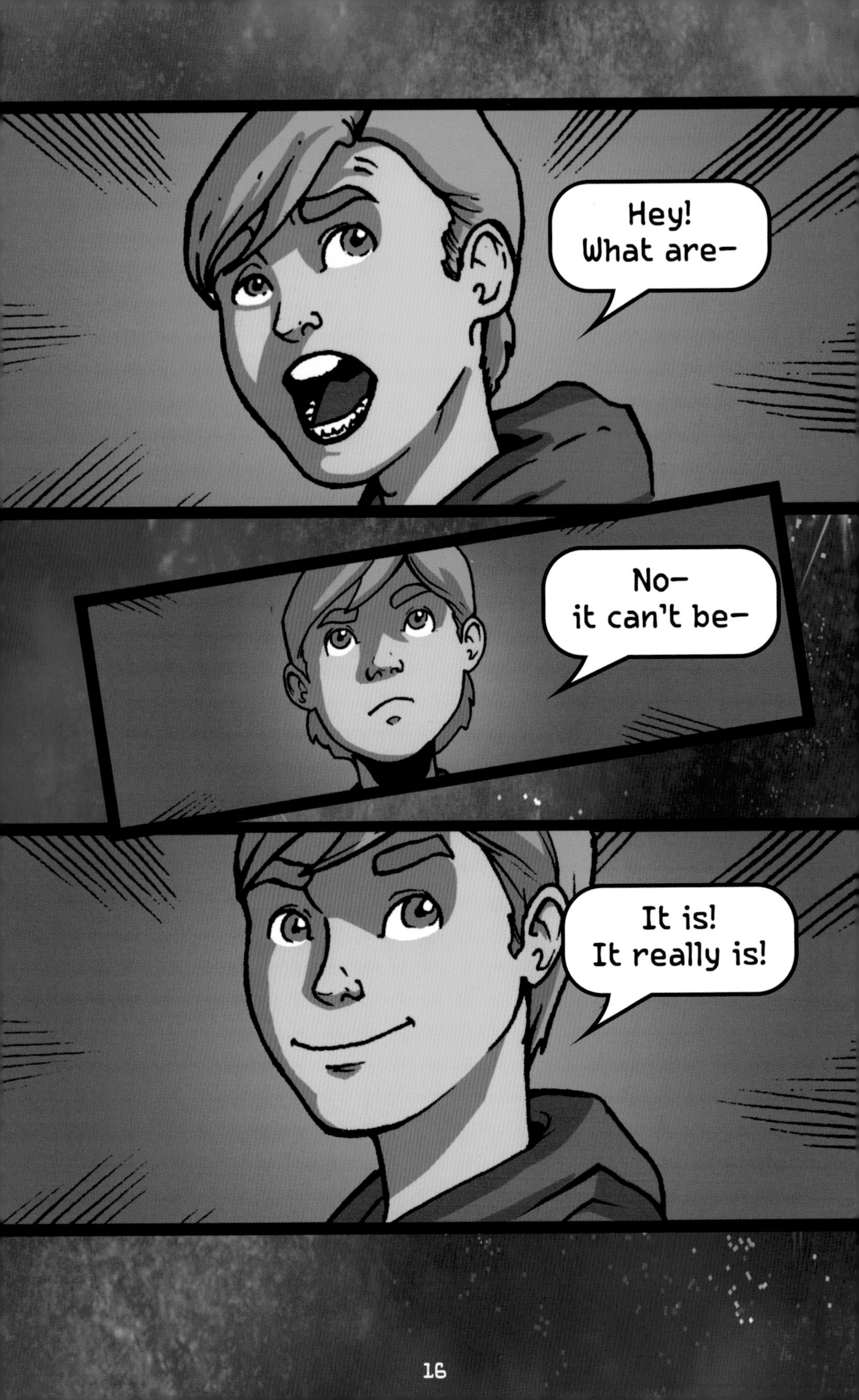
Hey! What are–
No– it can't be–
It is! It really is!

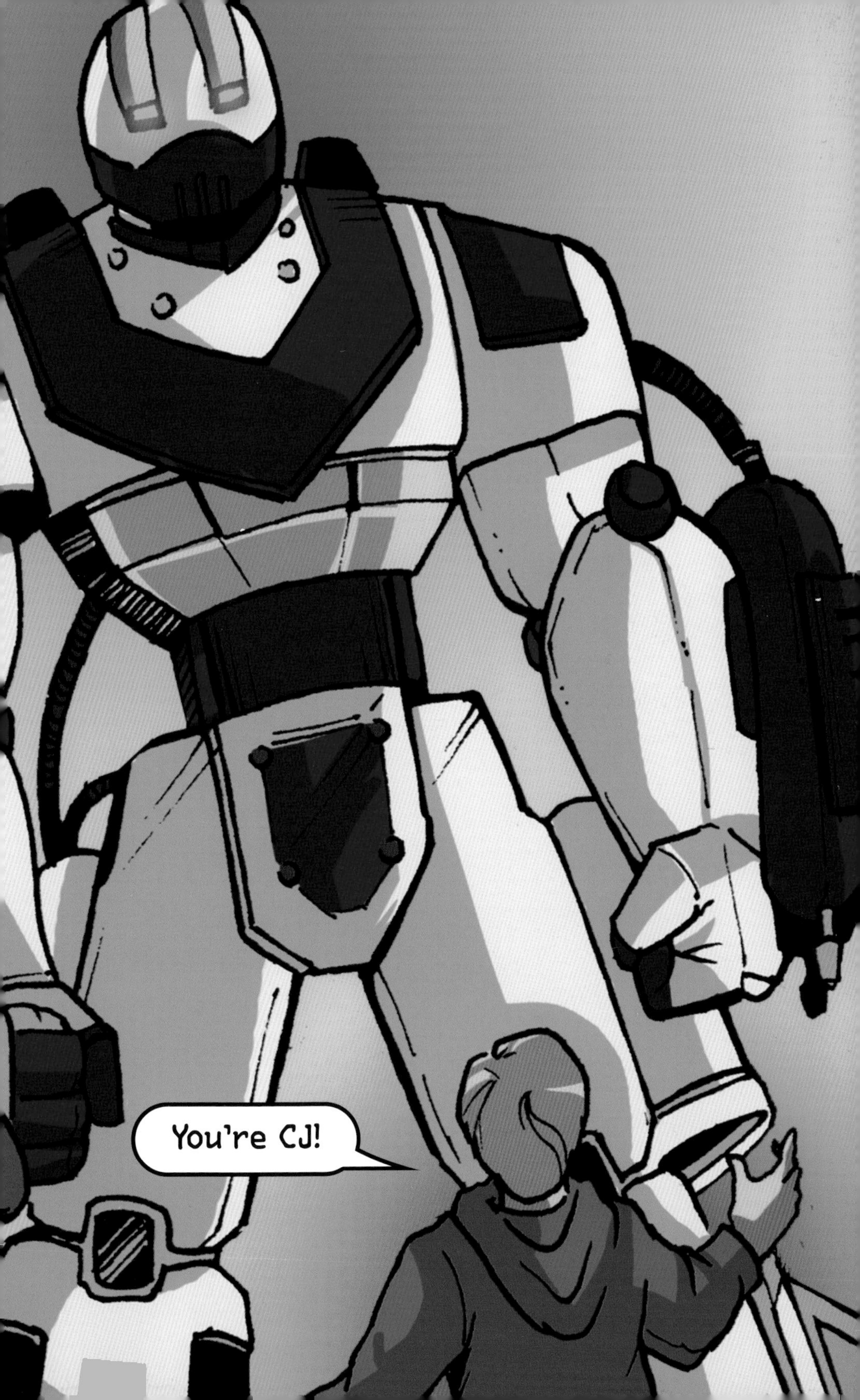
You're CJ!

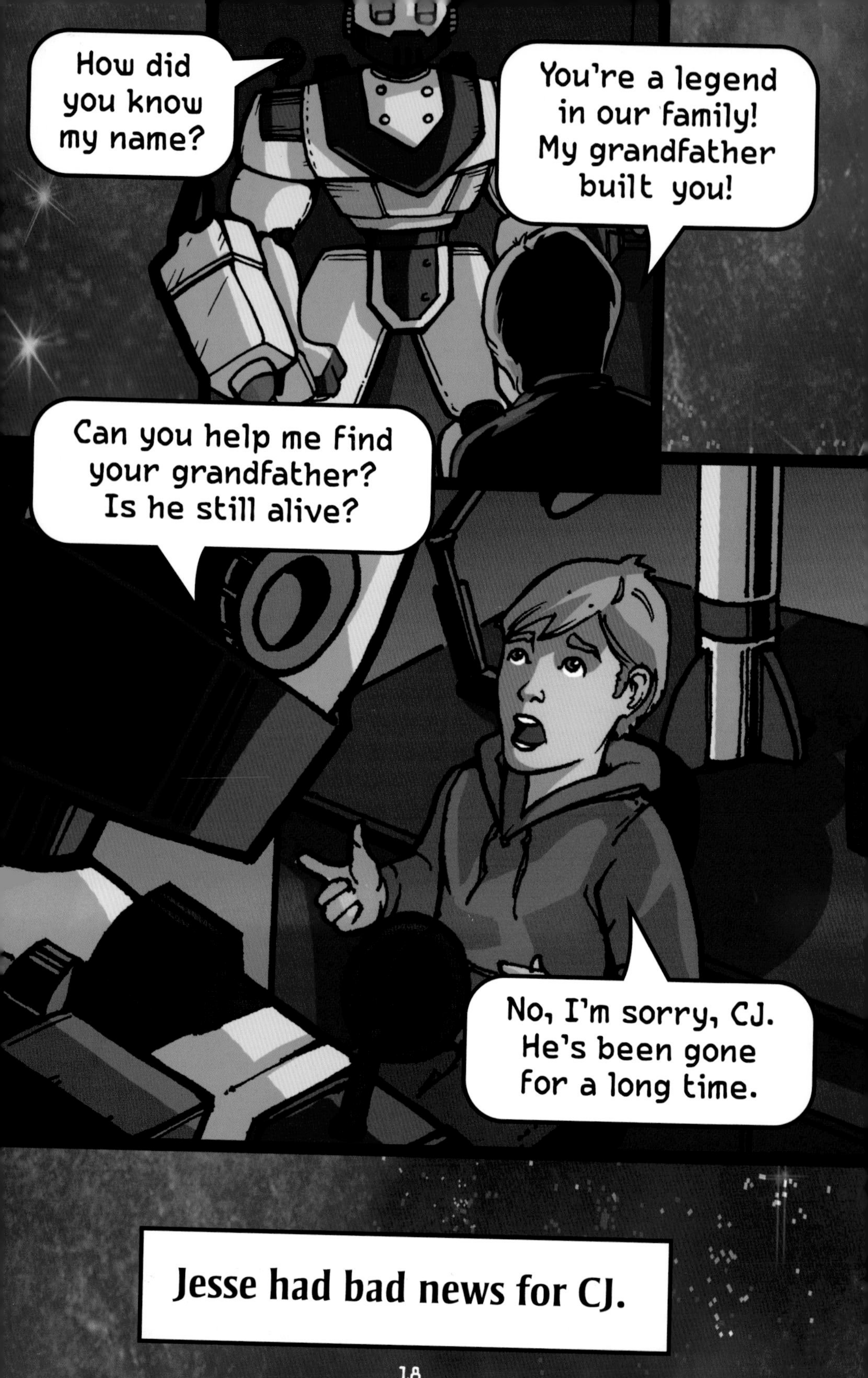
How did you know my name?
You're a legend in our family! My grandfather built you!
Can you help me find your grandfather? Is he still alive?
No, I'm sorry, CJ. He's been gone for a long time.
Jesse had bad news for CJ.

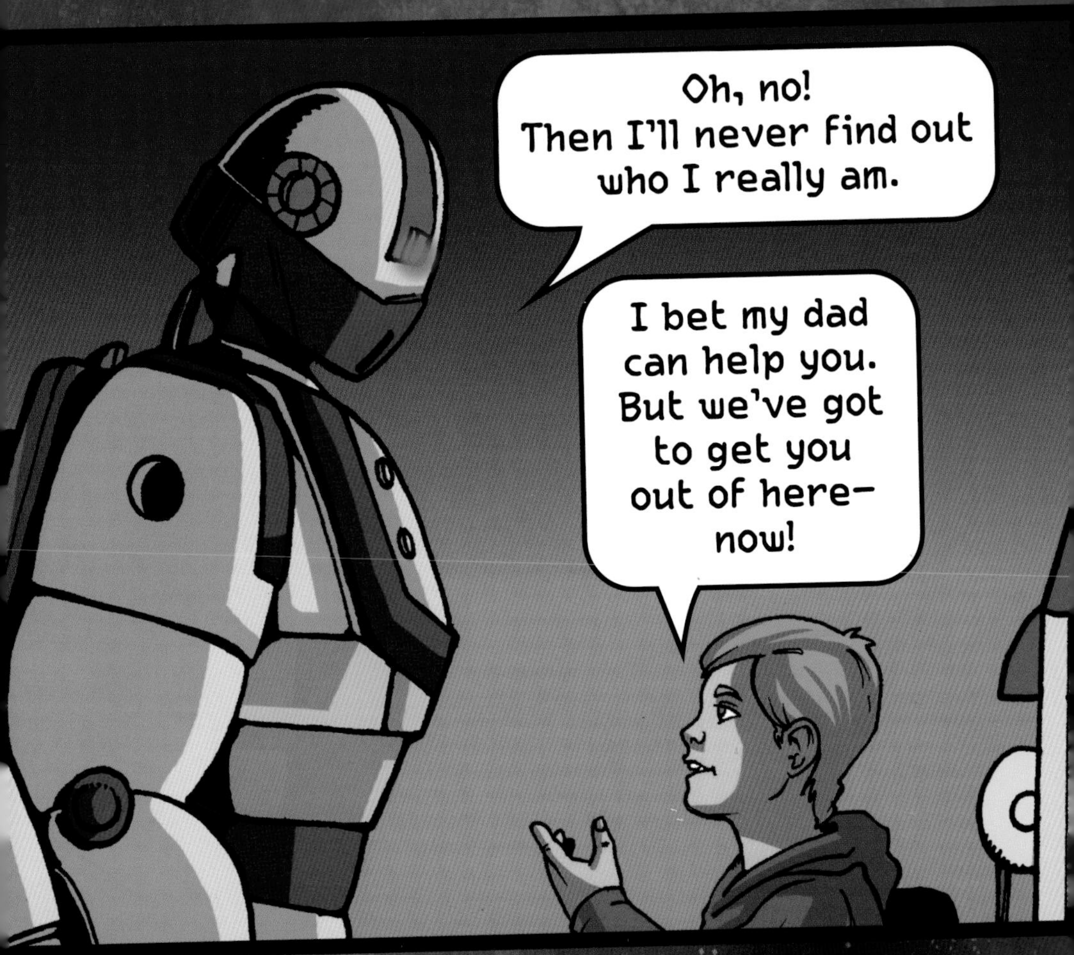
Oh, no! Then I'll never find out who I really am.
I bet my dad can help you. But we've got to get you out of here—now!

Jesse knew some scientists would want to experiment on CJ. He thought CJ would be safer at his house.

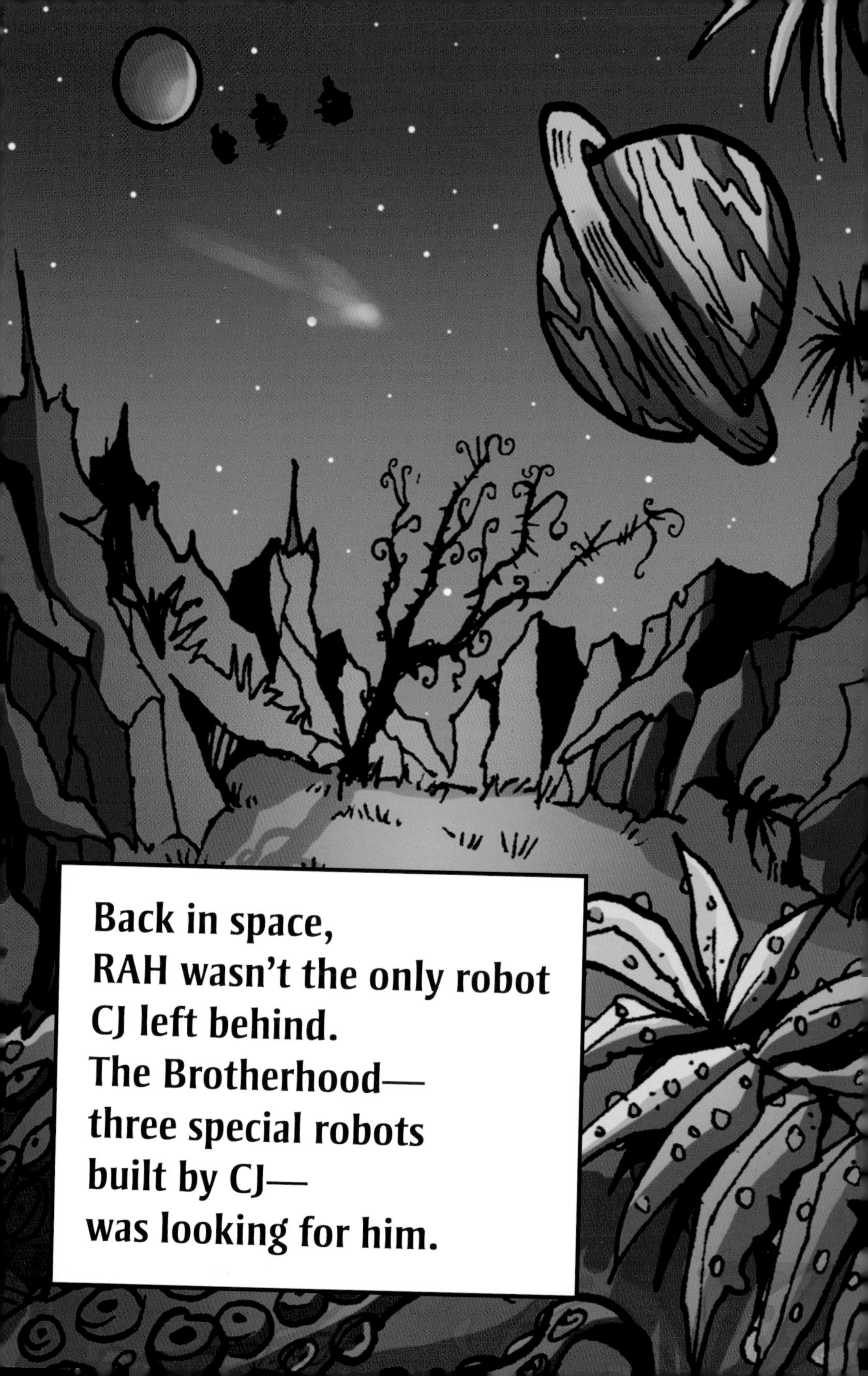
Back in space,
RAH wasn't the only robot
CJ left behind.
The Brotherhood—
three special robots
built by CJ—
was looking for him.

CARSON

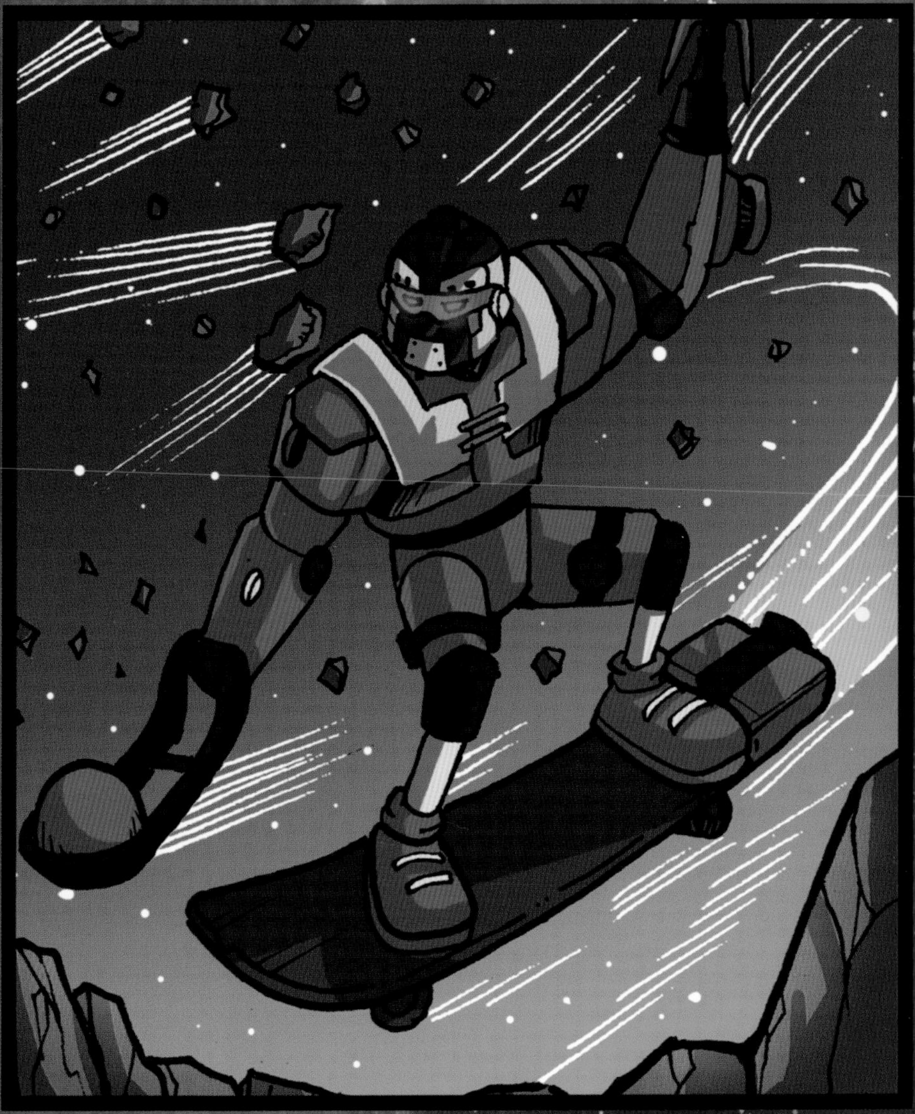

CREATED: 1978.
LOCATION: The Robot Galaxy.
BODY: Orange and silver.
EYES: Green.
TRAITS: Speed, independence, fearlessness.

PANGO

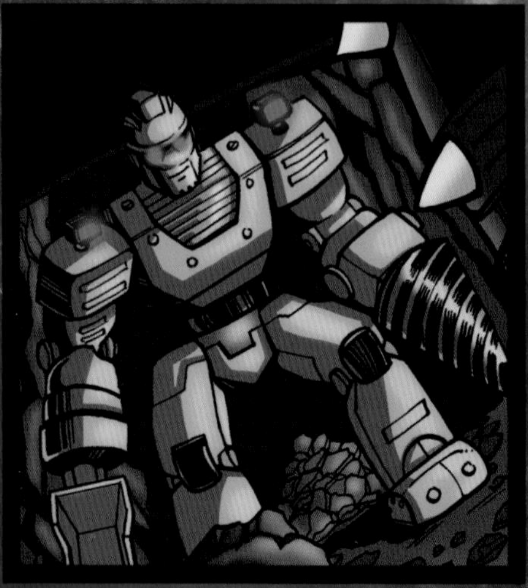

CREATED: 1975.
LOCATION:
The Robot Galaxy.
BODY: Yellow.
EYES: Green.
TRAITS: Building, exploring, creating.

JO

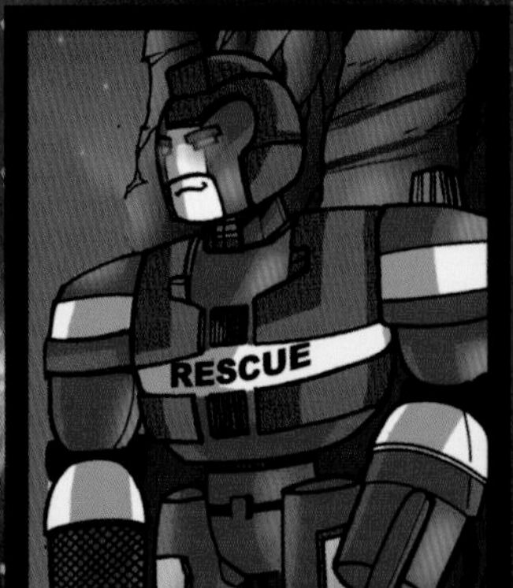
RESCUE

CREATED: 1973.
LOCATION:
The Robot Galaxy.
BODY: Red.
EYES: Green.
TRAITS: Rescue, teamwork, intelligence.

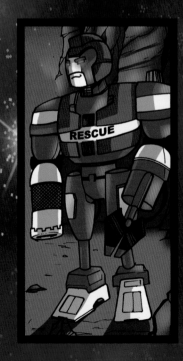

Carson, Pango, and Jo zoomed through space.

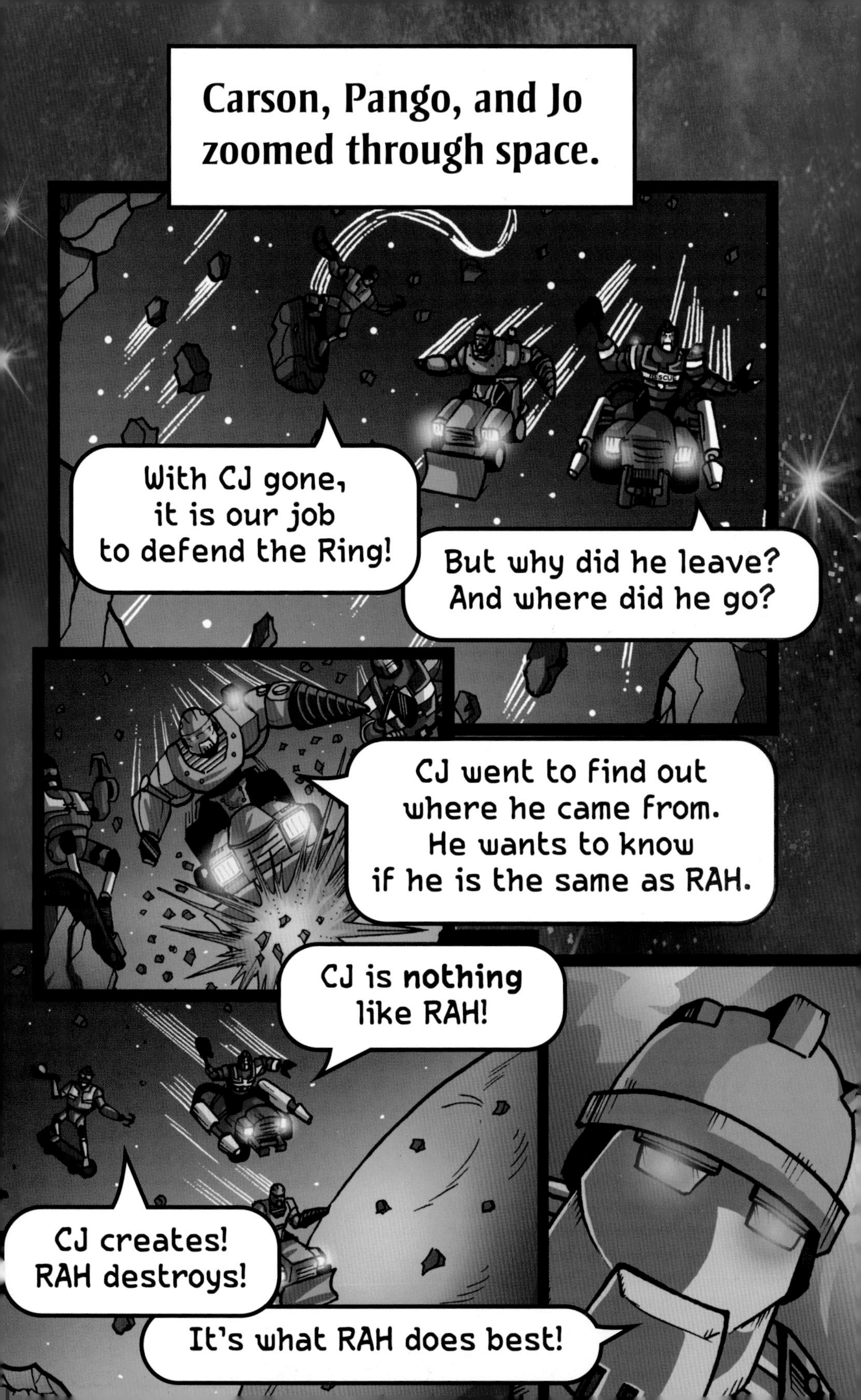
With CJ gone, it is our job to defend the Ring!
But why did he leave? And where did he go?
CJ went to find out where he came from. He wants to know if he is the same as RAH.
CJ is nothing like RAH!
CJ creates! RAH destroys!
It's what RAH does best!

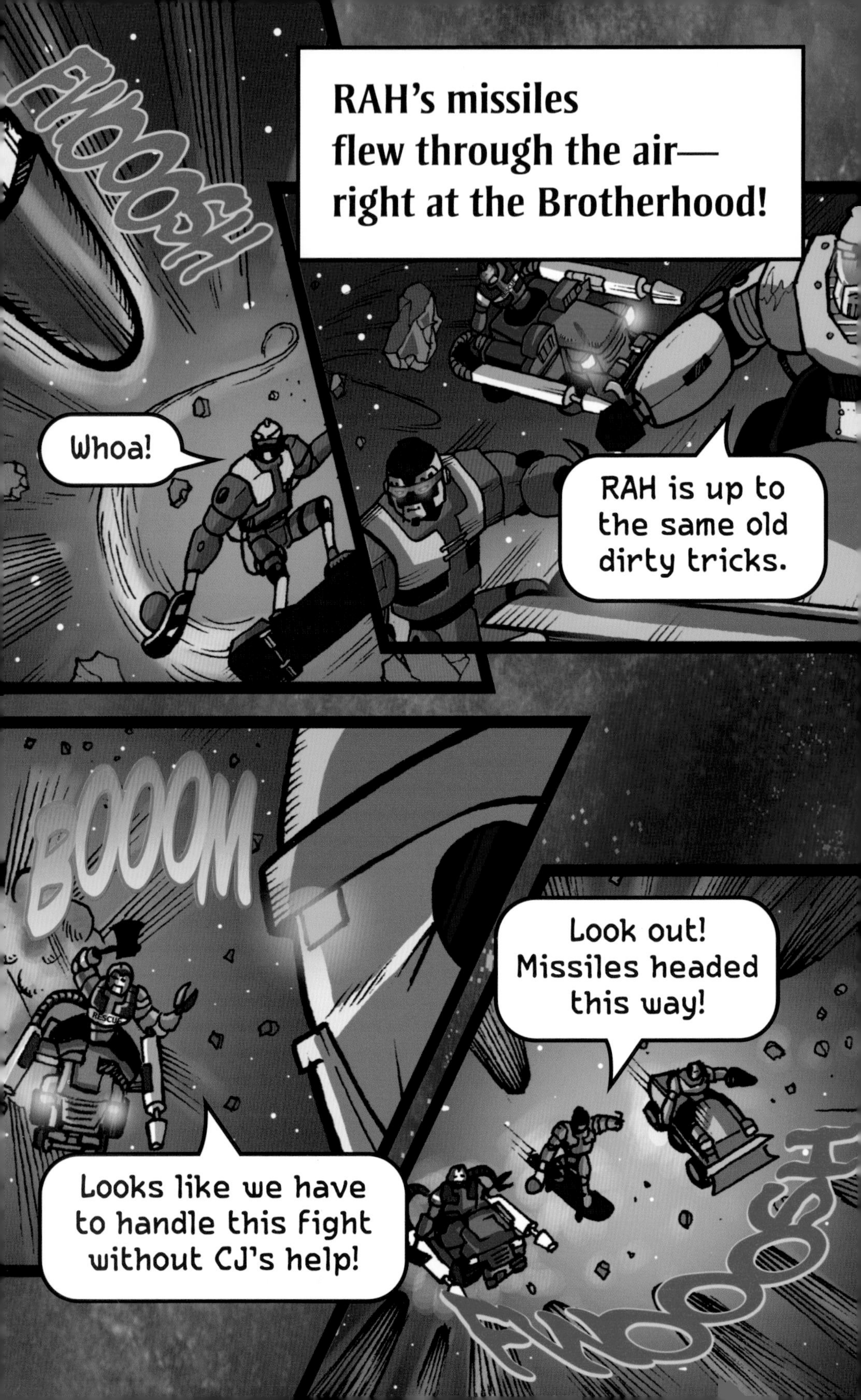
RAH's missiles flew through the air—right at the Brotherhood!
FWOOSH
Whoa!
RAH is up to the same old dirty tricks.
BOOOM
Looks like we have to handle this fight without CJ's help!
Look out! Missiles headed this way!
FWOOSH

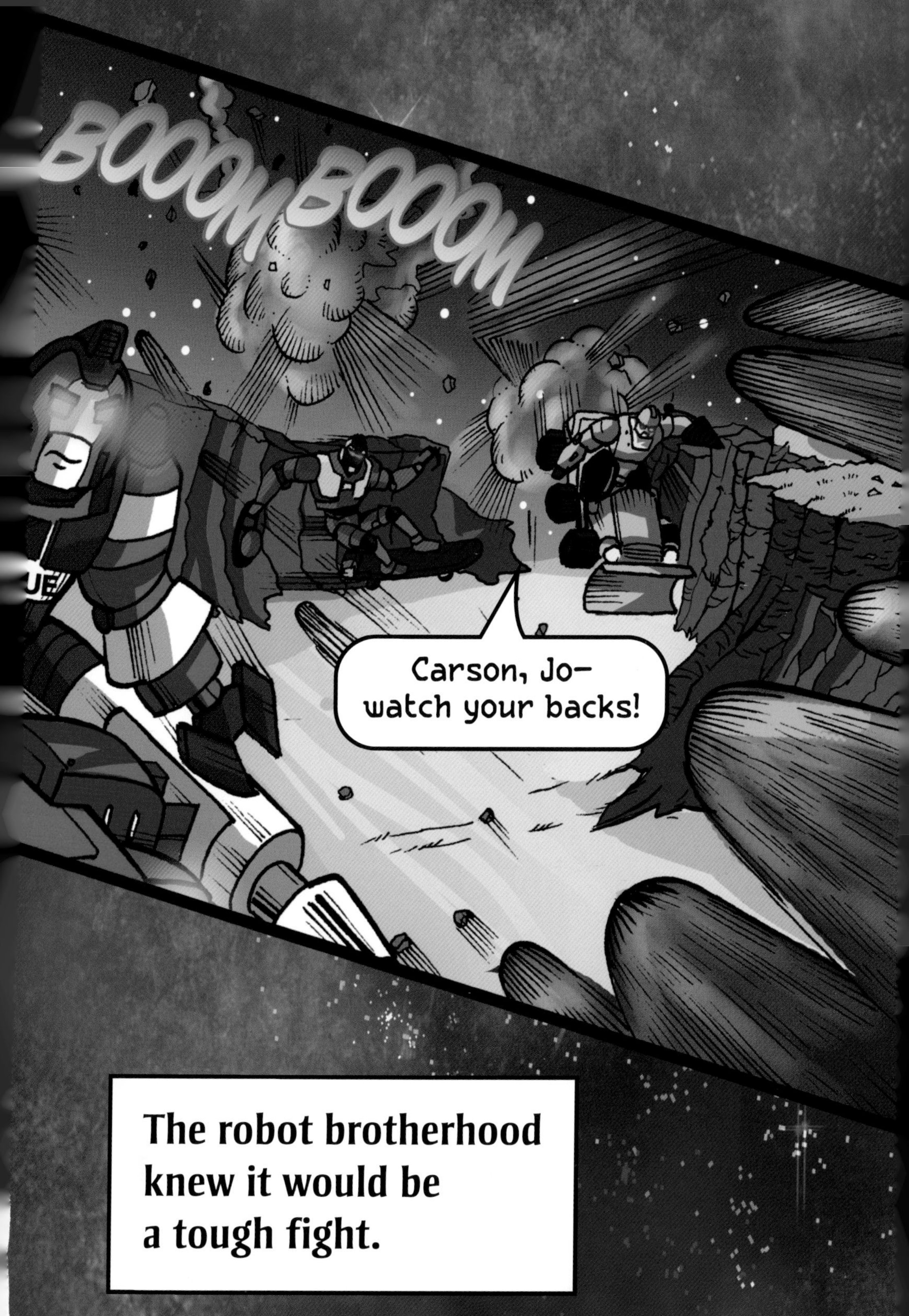
BOOOM BOOOM
Carson, Jo-watch your backs!
The robot brotherhood knew it would be a tough fight.

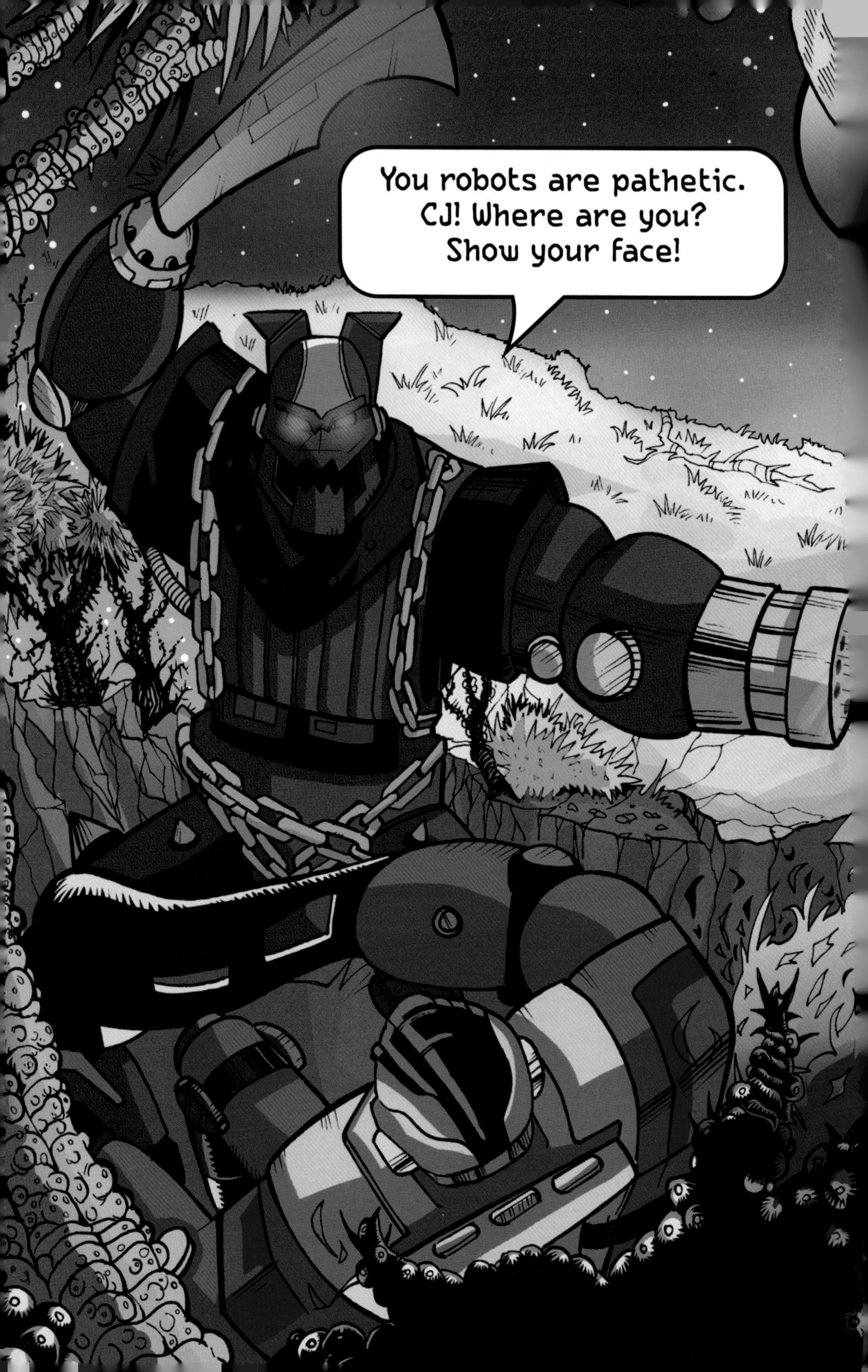
You robots are pathetic. CJ! Where are you? Show your face!

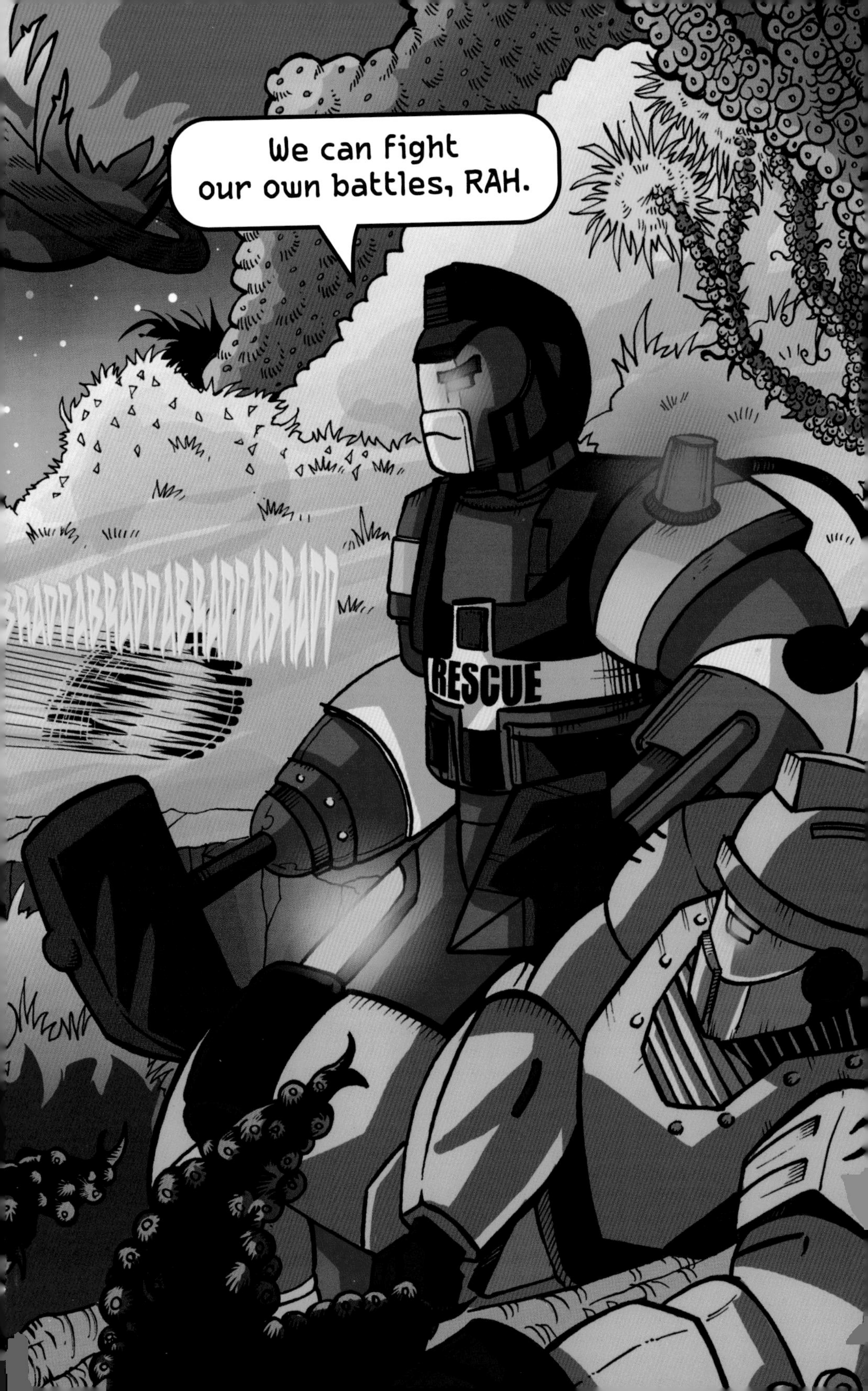
We can fight our own battles, RAH.
BRADDABRADDABRADDABRADD
RESCUE

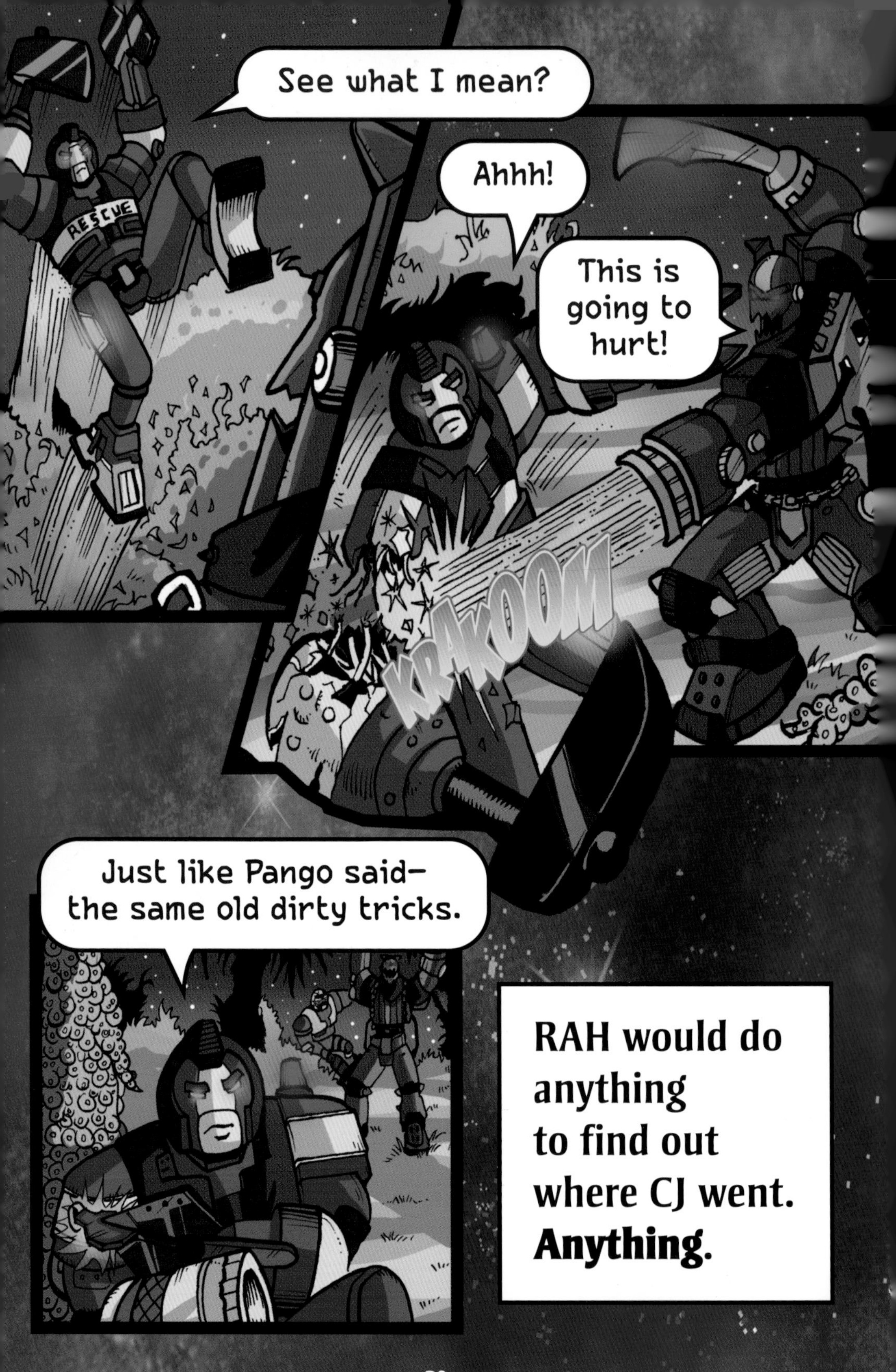
See what I mean?
Ahhh!
This is going to hurt!
KRAKOOM
Just like Pango said— the same old dirty tricks.
RAH would do anything to find out where CJ went. **Anything.**

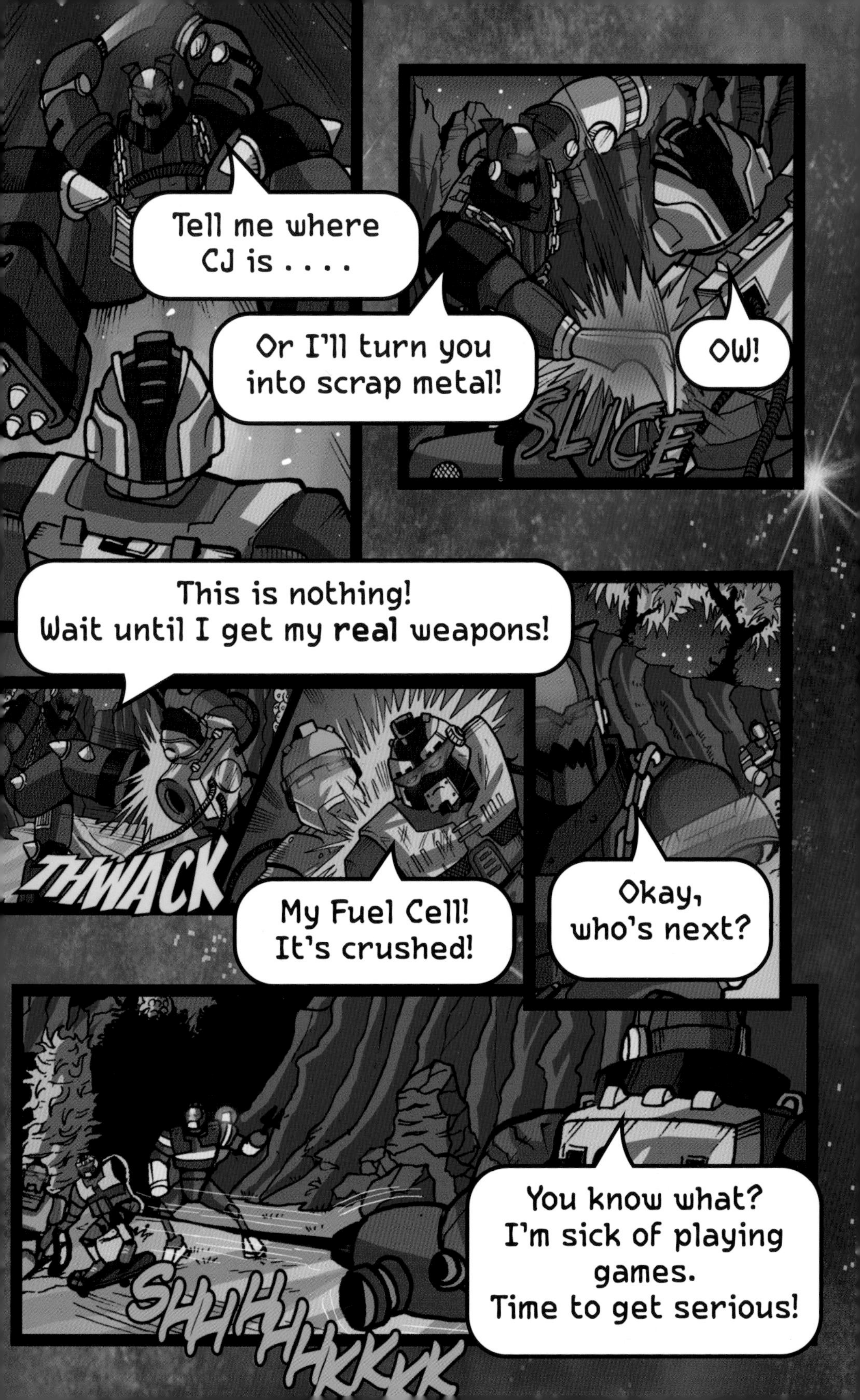
Tell me where CJ is . . . .
Or I'll turn you into scrap metal!
SLICE
OW!
This is nothing! Wait until I get my **real** weapons!
THWACK
My Fuel Cell! It's crushed!
Okay, who's next?
SHHHHKKKK
You know what? I'm sick of playing games. Time to get serious!

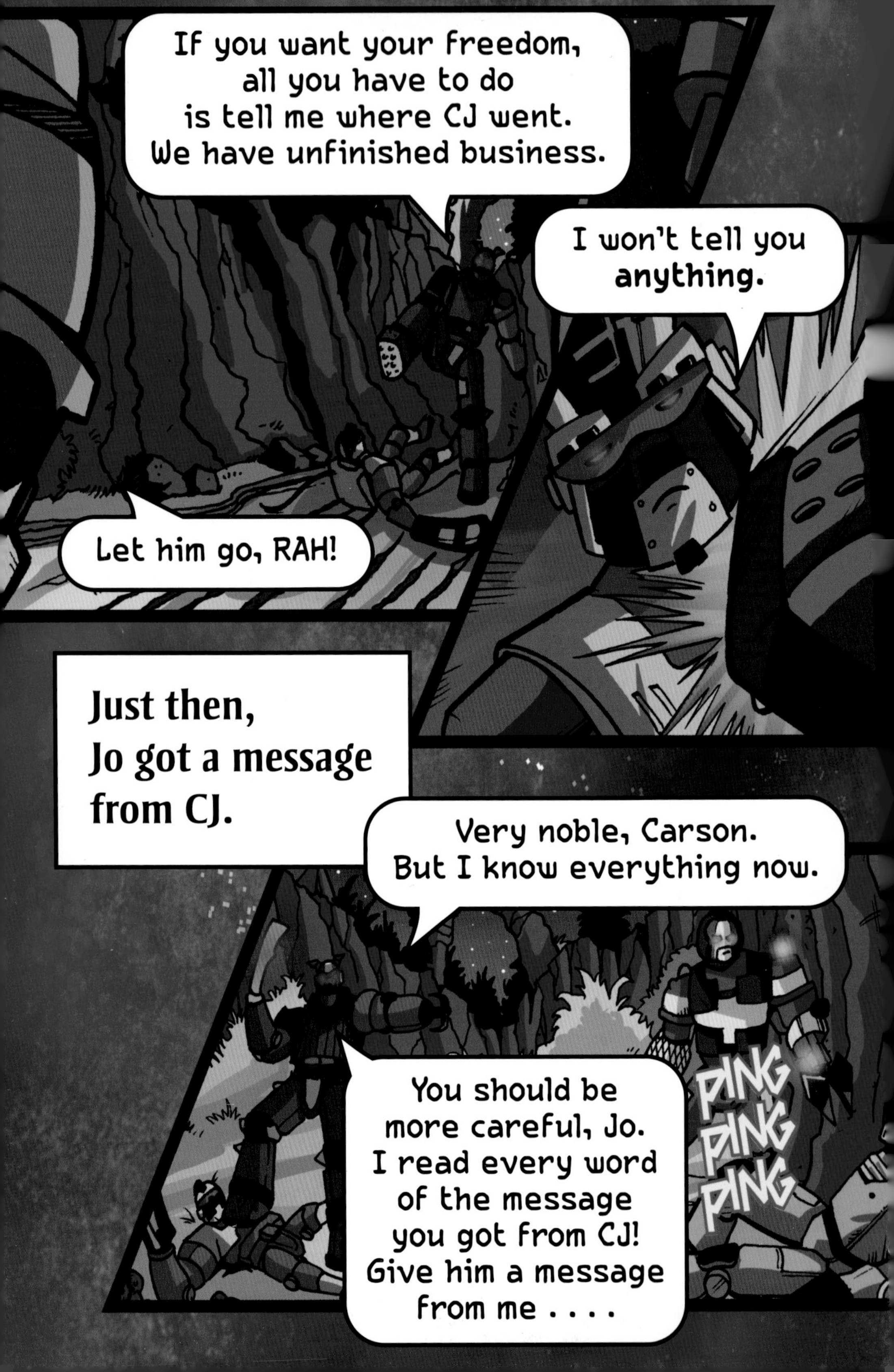
If you want your freedom, all you have to do is tell me where CJ went. We have unfinished business.
Let him go, RAH!
I won't tell you anything.
Just then, Jo got a message from CJ.
Very noble, Carson. But I know everything now.
You should be more careful, Jo. I read every word of the message you got from CJ! Give him a message from me . . . .
PING PING PING

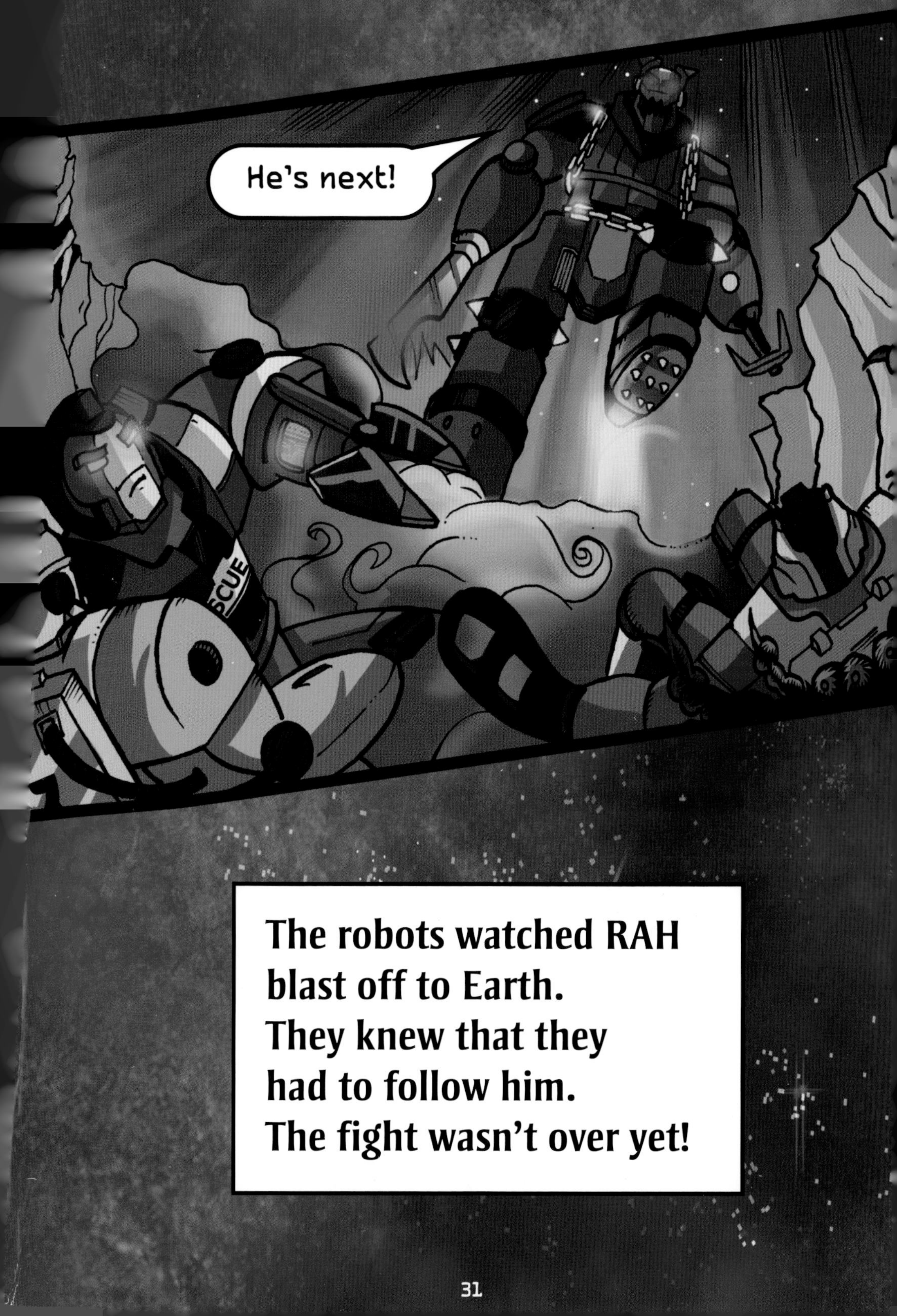
He's next!

The robots watched RAH
blast off to Earth.
They knew that they
had to follow him.
The fight wasn't over yet!